Hairs ⊙ Pelitos

by Sandra Cisneros · illustrated by Terry Ybáñez

TRES FLORES

three flowers
BRILLIANTINE
CONTAINS:
3¼ OZ. NET WT.   PETROLATUM, FRAGRANCE

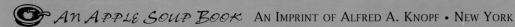

AN APPLE SOUP BOOK AN IMPRINT OF ALFRED A. KNOPF · NEW YORK

Para los kids,

Aleksandra,
Alfredito,
Alain,
Alonso,
Paolo,
Alexandro,
y Arturito

—S. C.

Para mis estudiantes de Travis
Elementary en San Antonio, Tejas

—T. Y.

———————————————

Translated from the English by Liliana Valenzuela

Traducción al español por Liliana Valenzuela

Everybody in our family has different hair.

Todos en nuestra familia tenemos pelo diferente.

My papa's hair is like a broom,

El pelo de mi papá es como una escoba,

all up in the air.

todo parado de punta.

And me, my hair is lazy.

Y yo, mi pelo es flojo.

It never obeys barrettes or bands.

Nunca obedece a broches o diademas.

Carlos's hair is thick and straight.

El pelo de Carlos es grueso y lacio.

He doesn't need to comb it.

No necesita peinárselo.

Nenny's hair is slippery—

El pelo de Nenny es resbaloso—

slides out of your hand.

se escurre de tu mano.

And Kiki, who is youngest,

Y Kiki, el más chiquito,

has hair like fur.

tiene pelo como peluche.

But my mother's hair, my mother's hair, like little rosettes,

Pero el pelo de mi mamá, el pelo de mi mamá, como rositas,

like little candy circles, all curly and pretty because

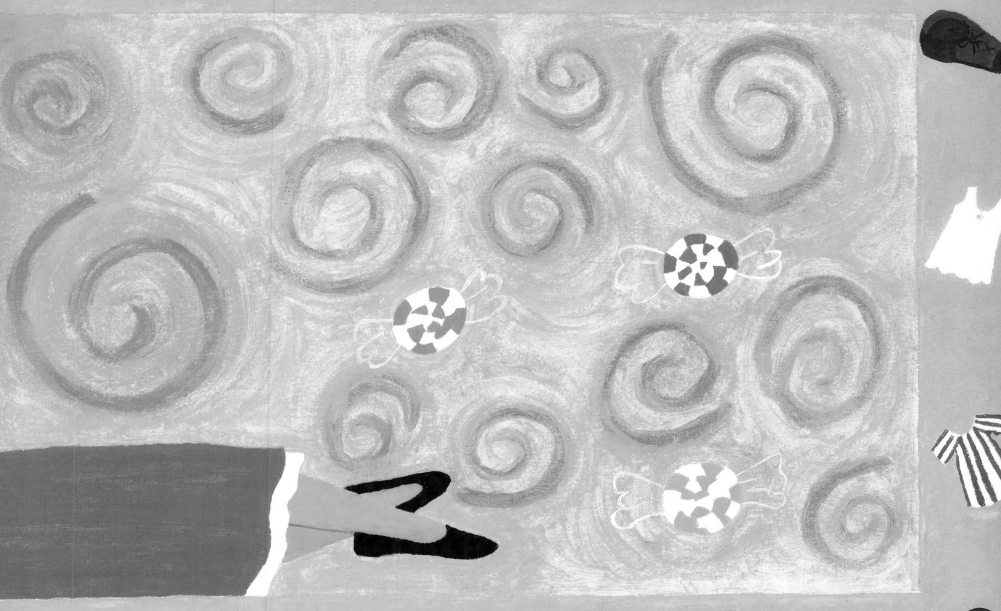

como rueditas de dulce, todas chinitas y lindas porque

she pinned it in pin curls all day,

GIL'S
Furniture

DRUG
STORE

JUNK
STORE

LAUNDROMAT

se hizo anchoas con pasadores todo el día,

sweet to put your nose into when she is holding you,

dulce cuando pones tu nariz en él cuando te abraza,

holding you and you feel safe,

cuando te abraza y te sientes segura,

is the warm smell of bread before you bake it,

es el olor tibio a pan antes de hornearlo,

is the smell when she makes room for you

es el olor cuando te hace un campito

on her side of the bed still warm with her skin,

en su lado de la cama todavía calientito de su piel,

and you sleep near her,

y te duermes cerca de ella,

the rain outside falling and Papa snoring.

la lluvia cayendo afuera y Papá roncando.

The snoring, the rain, and Mama's hair that smells like bread.

Los ronquidos, la lluvia, y el pelo de Mamá que huele a pan.

APPLE SOUP IS A TRADEMARK OF ALFRED A. KNOPF, INC.

Text copyright © 1984, 1994 by Sandra Cisneros
Illustrations copyright © 1994 by Terry Ybáñez

All rights reserved under International and Pan-American Copyright Conventions. Published in the United States of America by Alfred A. Knopf, Inc., New York, and simultaneously in Canada by Random House of Canada Limited, Toronto. Distributed by Random House, Inc., New York. The text in this work was originally published in 1984 by Arte Publico Press as part of the collection *The House on Mango Street.*

Library of Congress Cataloging-in-Publication Data

Cisneros, Sandra
Hairs = Pelitos / by Sandra Cisneros ; illustrated by Terry Ybáñez.
p.   cm.
An Apple Soup Book
Summary: A child describes how each person in the family has hair that looks and acts different, Papa's like a broom, Kiki's like fur, and Mama's with the smell of warm bread.
ISBN 0-679-86171-8 (trade) — ISBN 0-679-96171-2 (lib. bdg.)
[1. Hair—Fiction. 2. Hispanic Americans—Fiction. 3. Spanish language materials—Bilingual.]
I. Ybáñez, Terry, ill. II. Title. III. Title: Pelitos.
PZ73.C53   1994   93-32775

Manufactured in Singapore.
10 9 8 7 6 5 4 3 2 1